HISTORY SPEAKS

PICTURE BOOKS PLUS READER'S THEATER

Clara Morgan and the
OREGON TRAIL
JOURNEY

BY **MARTY RHODES FIGLEY**

ILLUSTRATED BY **CRAIG ORBACK**

M MILLBROOK PRESS / MINNEAPOLIS

For my wonderful sisters-in-law, Pat and Jane—both perfect biscuit bakers. MRF

For Jessica—Chicago, Minneapolis, the Badlands, Chimney Rock, Mount Rushmore, the Grand Tetons, Yellowstone, and Montana. What a time we had crossing America. With love, CO

Text copyright © 2011 by Marty Rhodes Figley
Illustrations copyright © 2011 by Craig Orback

Millbrook Press
A division of Lerner Publishing Group, Inc.
241 First Avenue North
Minneapolis, MN 55401 U.S.A.

Website address: www.lernerbooks.com

The illustrator gives special thanks to those who modeled for the various characters—especially Kelly Folkertsma as Clara; Kari Folkertsma as Iris; Sam Hunter as the twins Edwin and Seth; Finnegan Tait as Daniel; Annette Oyler Janzen as Mrs. Bell; and Jessica Silks, who modeled as Ma and helped with photography.

The publisher wishes to thank Professor Peter C. Mancall, University of Southern California, Departments of History and Anthropology and director of USC Huntington Early Modern Studies Institute, for serving as a consultant on this title.

The image in this book is used with the permission of: © Topham/The Image Works, p. 33.

Library of Congress Cataloging-in-Publication Data

Figley, Marty Rhodes, 1948-
    Clara Morgan and the Oregon Trail journey / by Marty Rhodes Figley ; illustrated by Craig Orback.
       p.   cm. — (History speaks: picture books plus reader's theater)
    Includes bibliographical references.
    ISBN 978-0-7613-5878-7 (lib. bdg. : alk. paper)
    1. Oregon National Historic Trail—Juvenile literature. 2. Overland journeys to the Pacific—Juvenile literature. 3. Frontier and pioneer life—West (U.S.)—Juvenile literature. I. Orback, Craig, ill. II. Title.
    F880.F46 2011
    978'.02—dc22   2010027431

Manufactured in the United States of America
1 – CG – 12/31/10

CONTENTS

THE OREGON TRAIL

◆ *June 1864* ◆

Plunk! Something hard hit eleven-year-old Clara Morgan's shoulder as she struggled to start a fire.

"Throw the biscuit to me—not Clara!" her brother Seth told his twin, Edwin.

"Stop it!" Clara yelled.

Seth got down on his knees and pretended to beg, "Clara, please, please, don't bake any more of those biscuits!"

Edwin pulled another one from his pocket. He tossed it into the air. "Sorry, Clara, but they taste terrible. All these are good for is playing catch!"

Clara's eyes filled with tears. She wished Iris were here to help. But her sister was busy taking care of Ma and their two-year-old brother, Daniel. Ma was expecting a baby soon, and she had taken poorly last week. Until Ma felt better, it was Clara's job to do the cooking.

Back home in Springfield, Missouri, Clara had been a good cook. But baking on an open fire was hard. Her biscuits always burned.

A huge raindrop plopped on Clara's cheek. Good, she thought, it will hide the tears. The wind whipped up and then something else hit Clara's head. Hail, big as hen's eggs.

"Don't just stand there with your hands in your pockets!" she yelled. "Grab the pans and run for the wagon!"

Pa was close behind them. A canvas tent was pitched beside the wagon. Inside, Ma was propped up on a feather mattress, holding little Daniel. Iris passed out tin plates. Clara served up crackers, beef jerky, and dried apples. There would be no more cooking outside tonight.

Seth poked a slice of dried apple into his mouth. "One thing's for sure," he said. "When we eat these for supper, they swell up in my stomach and keep me full for quite a spell."

Everyone laughed. Clara thought it was like a cozy picnic, with the whole family gathered inside the tent. The storm raged outside.

Seth said, "Did you see the Indians ride by our camp just before the storm started?"

"They didn't stop," Pa replied. "If they come back, it will probably be to trade."

For over twenty years, pioneers following their dreams had traveled to Oregon on the Oregon Trail. Clara's family was doing the same. The trail cut through Indian Territory. As more and more travelers passed through, they trampled the Indians' land. They also shot many buffalo. The buffalo was sacred to the Indians, who depended on the animal for its meat and hide. Sometimes violence broke out.

Iris said, "I hope there's no trouble."
"If we respect the Indians, they'll respect us," said Pa.
Clara hoped he was right.

The next morning, the twins took off early and returned with sloshing pails. "Here's your day's supply of some nice muddy Platte River water, Clara," said Seth. "And I milked Bessie," said Edwin. Her brothers' smiles were sweet. Clara almost forgave them for yesterday.

Seth announced, "It's now one month and twenty-eight days since we left Independence!" He had carved a mark on the wagon for each day they traveled.

"When we reach Fort Laramie, we will have traveled 650 miles!" said Edwin.

Clara had no time to think about the miles. Once again, she struggled with her cooking. The fire was fine for frying bacon and boiling coffee. But it burned her bread. Mrs. Bell, a nice lady who was traveling to Oregon with her sons, stopped by to visit.

Clara said, "I wish I could bake biscuits like Ma."

"Come by tonight," said Mrs. Bell. "I'll show you a trick or two."

Clara spent a dusty day walking beside the oxen. She tried to keep their dog, Shep, from pestering the big, gentle animals that pulled their wagon. By late afternoon, the wagon train had camped.

Clara stared at the endless prairie. How she longed to sit under a shady tree with a cool glass of lemonade!

Instead, she wandered over to Mrs. Bell's campfire. Mrs. Bell smiled at Clara. "You're just in time!" she said. "Let's bake." Mrs. Bell put biscuit dough in a heavy iron pot with a lid, called a Dutch oven. She showed Clara how to use little fires of sagebrush twigs under the pot and on top of the lid. Then Clara could control the fire more so her bread wouldn't burn.

The next afternoon, Clara decided to make biscuits for dinner.
If they were good, they would surely cheer Ma. Clara traded
some of Bessie's milk for one of Mrs. Bell's chicken's eggs to
make the biscuits richer. She baked them as Mrs. Bell had
showed her. Clara smiled as she opened the lid of the
Dutch oven to peek. Her biscuits were golden brown,
not black! It would be beans with hot biscuits
and molasses for dinner tonight.

The family gathered 'round. Seth said, "I can't
believe you made these biscuits!"
"They look perfect!" said Ma.
Edwin glanced toward another wagon.
He whispered, "What's he doing?"

Clara saw an Indian dressed
in buckskin making his way from
campfire to campfire. People at
wagon after wagon turned him
away. Then he looked toward
Clara's wagon.

He walked over and pointed to
Clara's biscuits. "I am hungry," he
said. Clara was surprised he knew
how to speak her language. She
surely didn't know how to speak his.

She handed him a hot biscuit on a plate. She set the can of molasses beside him. The Indian squatted on the ground. He poured molasses on the biscuit. Then he delicately pulled it apart with his fingers and ate it. The Indian pointed at the pan.

Clara looked at Pa. He nodded. She gave the Indian the rest of the biscuits.

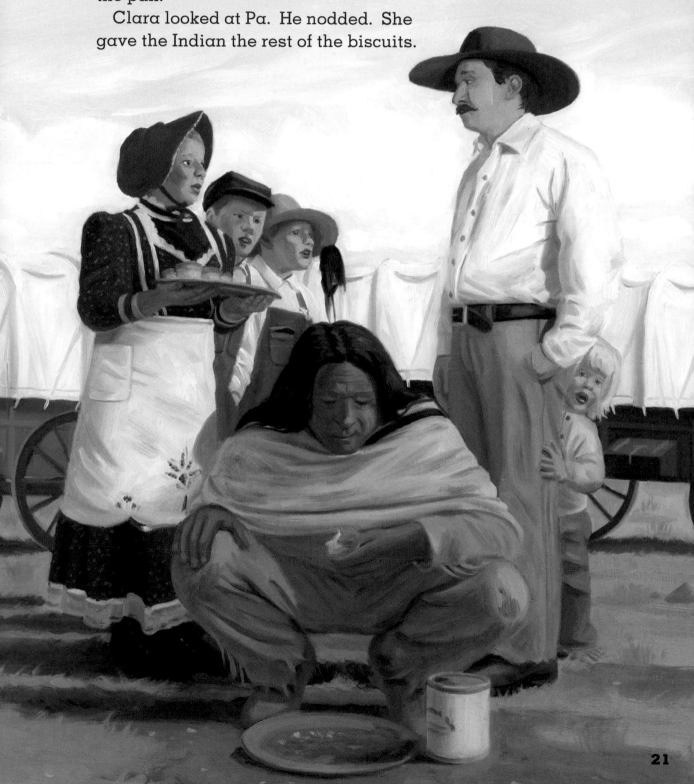

He ate all but three. He tucked them into his buckskin shirt.
"For hungry papooses," he said.
He stood up and looked at Pa. "Your family?" he asked.
Pa said, "Yes."

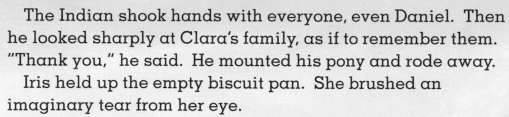

The Indian shook hands with everyone, even Daniel. Then he looked sharply at Clara's family, as if to remember them. "Thank you," he said. He mounted his pony and rode away.

Iris held up the empty biscuit pan. She brushed an imaginary tear from her eye.

They all laughed. A meal of beans and bacon with some hard crackers would have to do.

The next morning, the Morgan wagon led the wagon train. Each family took turns. It was less dusty at the front than farther back. Clara walked beside Pa and the oxen.

Soon a long line of Indians appeared in the distance. Their faces were painted. They yelled and shook their tomahawks as they rode closer.

The wagon train halted. Men grabbed their rifles, ready
to fight.

A lone Indian suddenly appeared. He galloped his pony
in front of the warriors with his hand raised. He must have
been their leader, because the other Indians stopped. They
turned and rode away.

Pa said, "I don't know why, but I think just now we were
powerful lucky."

Clara gulped. "When will we reach Fort Laramie?" she asked.

"In about three days," said Pa. "We'll stay a spell to do repairs and buy supplies. There's a doctor at the fort that your ma can see."

Clara was glad that the Indians didn't show up again before they reached the fort.

Fort Laramie bustled with crowds of travelers, soldiers, and Indians. The family camped outside the fort. During supper, Clara delighted in watching all the people. She saw an Indian coming toward them. He wore beautifully beaded, creamy white buckskin. His feather headdress reached to his heels. A group of Indians followed him.

"Don't you recognize him?" whispered Seth. Clara gasped. He was the Indian who had eaten all their biscuits!

The Indian smiled and said, "Friends." He shook hands solemnly with everyone again. Then he told Pa about a good place close by to hunt for elk.

After a few minutes, he raised his hand in a farewell gesture. He left, followed by the other Indians.

A soldier standing nearby smiled and asked, "Entertaining royalty, are you?"

"What do you mean?" asked Pa.

"That man you were just talking to is a powerful Indian in these parts. He's one of the most respected leaders in the Sioux Nation. You could have a worse man for a friend."

Pa and Clara looked at each other. Could that be the reason they hadn't been attacked a few days ago?

Edwin said, "He's our friend because of Clara's biscuits!" The soldier looked confused.

Pa laughed and said, "It's a long story."

Two days later, while they were still at Fort Laramie, Clara's new baby sister arrived. Ma and Pa named her Evalina.

On their last night at Fort Laramie, Clara pulled another pan of perfect biscuits off the fire. Ma was feeling better every day. Soon she would start cooking again. But Clara knew one thing for certain. No matter what, she would keep baking her lucky biscuits all the way to Oregon!

Author's Note

From 1841 to 1870, more than 250,000 people left their homes and traveled the Oregon Trail. This route stretched from Missouri to Oregon and the Pacific Northwest. Travelers went in search of adventure, fortune, land, gold, and even good weather. Parents dreamed of building a new life for themselves and their children.

Clara and her family were not real. But most of the things that happened to them in this book are based on real events. These stories came from the memories and diaries of people who traveled the Oregon Trail. The story about meeting one of the leaders in the Lakota Nation (called Sioux by white travelers) was true for one family along the trail. Mrs. Bell's bread-baking tip was really used too.

Sometimes children like Clara took on adult jobs when their parents were busy or ill. Many children on the Oregon Trail did chores like milking cows (if they were lucky enough to have them). They might have also fetched water, found fuel for the fire, and washed dishes and clothes. Children helped take care of the livestock that made the trip too. Animals such as oxen, horses, and mules were used for transportation. Cows, goats, and chickens were sometimes brought along to provide food.

In Clara's time, American Indians were often called Indians. Today they are called American Indians, Native Americans, or indigenous people. Most American Indians identify themselves by their tribe.

A GROUP OF LAKOTA VISIT FORT LARAMIE IN WYOMING IN 1868

The American Indians and the Oregon Trail travelers sometimes got along. Other times, they did not. It depended on the time and place. In many cases, American Indians offered information, food, equipment, and transportation help to Oregon Trail travelers. In 1851, the U.S. government and several American Indian nations signed the Treaty of Fort Laramie. The treaty said that travelers would be allowed to pass safely through Indian Territory. The U.S. government could also build forts and roads on Indian land. In exchange, the government would pay money to those American Indian nations each year.

By 1864, when Clara's family traveled the trail, more and more settlers had broken the treaty. They had made their homes on Indian land. They killed buffalo wastefully. In turn, American Indians became concerned about the number of people invading their territory. At times, violence broke out. As the Oregon Trail pioneers journeyed to a new land, it was often at great cost to the American Indians. Some settlers and American Indians formed friendships, as in this story. But because of the movement west, many groups of American Indians lost the land they had lived on for hundreds of years.

Performing Reader's Theater

Dear Student,

Reader's Theater is a dramatic reading. It is a little like a play, but you don't need to memorize your lines. Here are some tips that will help you do your best in a Reader's Theater performance.

BEFORE THE PERFORMANCE

- **Choose your part:** Your teacher may assign parts, or you may be allowed to choose your own part. The character you play does not need to be the same age as you. A boy can play the part of a girl, and a girl can play the part of a boy. That's why it's called acting!

- **Find your lines:** Your character's name is always the same color. The name at the bottom of each page tells you which character has the first line on the next page. If you are allowed to write on your script, highlight your lines. If you cannot write on the script, you may want to use sticky flags to mark your lines.

- **Check pronunciations of words:** If your character's lines include any words you aren't sure how to pronounce, check the pronunciation guide on page 45. If a word isn't there or you still aren't sure how to say it, check a dictionary or ask a teacher, librarian, or other adult.

- **Use your emotions:** Think about how your character feels in the story. If you imagine how your character feels, the audience will hear the emotion in your voice.

- **Use your imagination:** Think about how your character's voice might sound. For example, an old man's voice will sound different from a baby's voice. If you do change your voice, make sure the audience can still understand the words you are saying.

- **Practice your lines:** Even though you do not need to memorize your lines, you should still be comfortable reading them. Read your lines aloud often so they flow smoothly.

DURING THE PERFORMANCE

- **Keep your script away from your face but high enough to read:** If you cover your face with your script, you block your voice from the audience. If you have your script too low, you need to tip your head down farther to read it and the audience won't be able to hear you.

- **Use eye contact:** Good Reader's Theater performers look at the audience as much as they look at their scripts. If you look down, the sound of your voice goes down to the script and not out to the audience.

- **Speak clearly:** Make sure you are loud enough. Say all your words carefully. Be sure not to read too quickly. Remember, if you feel nervous, you may start to speak faster than usual.

- **Use facial expressions and gestures:** Your facial expressions and gestures (hand movements) help the audience know how your character is feeling. If your character is happy, smile. If your character is angry, cross your arms and be sure not to smile.

- **Have fun:** It's okay if you feel nervous. If you make a mistake, just try to relax and keep going. Reader's Theater is meant to be fun for the actors and the audience!

Cast of Characters

NARRATOR 1

NARRATOR 2

NARRATOR 3

SETH MORGAN

CLARA MORGAN

READER 1:
Edwin Morgan, Pa Morgan

READER 2:
Ma Morgan, Mrs. Bell

READER 3:
the Indian, the soldier

ALL:
Everyone except sound

SOUND:
This part has no lines. The person in this role
is in charge of the sound effects.
Find the sound effects for this script
at www.lerneresource.com.

The Script

NARRATOR 1: The year was 1864. Eleven-year-old Clara Morgan and her family stopped to rest on their way along the Oregon Trail that June.

SOUND: [plunk]

NARRATOR 2: Something hard hit Clara's shoulder as she struggled to start a fire.

SETH MORGAN: Eddie, throw the biscuit to me—not Clara!

CLARA MORGAN: Seth! Edwin! Stop it!

NARRATOR 3: Seth got down on his knees and pretended to beg.

SETH: Clara, please, please, don't bake any more of those biscuits!

NARRATOR 1: Edwin pulled another one from his pocket. He tossed it into the air.

READER 1 (as Edwin Morgan): Sorry, Clara, but they taste terrible. All these are good for is playing catch!

NARRATOR 2: Clara's eyes filled with tears. She wished Iris were here to help. But her sister was in the wagon, taking care of Ma and their two-year-old brother, Daniel. Ma was expecting a baby soon, and she had taken poorly last week. Until Ma felt better, it was Clara's job to do the cooking.

Next Page — **NARRATOR 3**

NARRATOR 3: Back home in Springfield, Missouri, Clara had been a good cook. But baking on an open fire was hard. Her biscuits always burned.

NARRATOR 1: A huge raindrop plopped on Clara's cheek.

CLARA: Good. The rain will hide my tears.

NARRATOR 2: The wind whipped up, and then something else hit Clara's head. Hail, big as hen's eggs.

SOUND: [wind blowing]

CLARA: Don't just stand there with your hands in your pockets! Grab the pans and run for the wagon!

NARRATOR 3: Pa was close behind them. A canvas tent was pitched beside the wagon. Inside, Ma was propped up on a feather mattress, holding little Daniel.

NARRATOR 1: Iris passed out tin plates. Clara served up crackers, beef jerky, and dried apples. There would be no more cooking outside tonight. Seth poked a slice of dried apple into his mouth.

SETH: One thing's for sure. When we eat these for supper, they swell up in my stomach and keep me full for quite a spell.

NARRATOR 2: Everyone laughed. Clara thought it was like a cozy picnic, with the whole family gathered inside the tent. The storm raged outside.

SOUND: [rain and thunder]

Next Page — **SETH**

SETH: Did you see the Indians ride by our camp just before the storm started?

READER 1 (as Pa Morgan): They didn't stop. If they come back, it will probably be to trade.

NARRATOR 3: For over twenty years, pioneers following their dreams had traveled to Oregon on the trail. Clara's family was doing the same. The Oregon Trail cut through Indian Territory. As more and more travelers passed through, they trampled the Indians' land.

NARRATOR 1: The travelers also shot many buffalo. The buffalo was sacred to the Indians, who depended on the animal for its meat and hide. Sometimes violence broke out.

READER 2 (as Ma Morgan): I hope there's no trouble.

READER 1 (AS PA): If we respect the Indians, they'll respect us.

CLARA: I hope he's right.

NARRATOR 2: The next morning, the twins took off early and returned with sloshing pails.

SETH: Here's your day's supply of nice, muddy Platte River water, Clara.

READER 1 (as Edwin): And I milked Bessie.

NARRATOR 3: Her brothers' smiles were sweet. Clara almost forgave them for yesterday.

SETH: It's now one month and twenty-eight days since we left Independence!

Next Page — **NARRATOR 1**

NARRATOR 1: Seth had carved a mark on the wagon for each day they traveled.

READER 1 (as Edwin): When we reach Fort Laramie, we will have traveled 650 miles!

NARRATOR 2: Clara had no time to think about the miles. Once again, she struggled with her cooking.

SOUND: [bacon sizzling]

NARRATOR 3: The fire was fine for frying bacon and boiling coffee. But the fire burned her bread. Mrs. Bell, a nice lady who was traveling to Oregon with her sons, stopped by to visit.

CLARA: I wish I could bake biscuits like Ma.

READER 2 (as Mrs. Bell): Come by tonight. I'll show you a trick or two.

NARRATOR 1: Clara spent a dusty day walking beside the oxen. She tried to keep their dog, Shep, from pestering the animals that pulled their wagon. By late afternoon, the wagon train had camped.

NARRATOR 2: Clara stared at the endless prairie. How she longed for a cool glass of lemonade! Instead, she wandered over to Mrs. Bell's campfire. Mrs. Bell smiled at Clara.

READER 2 (as Mrs. Bell): You're just in time! Let's bake. We'll put the biscuit dough in the Dutch oven.

NARRATOR 3: Mrs. Bell showed Clara how to use little fires of twigs under the heavy pot and on top of the lid. Then Clara could control the fire so her bread wouldn't burn.

Next Page — **NARRATOR 1**

NARRATOR 1: The next afternoon, Clara decided to make biscuits for dinner. If they were good, they would surely cheer Ma. Clara traded some of Bessie's milk for one of Mrs. Bell's chicken's eggs to make the biscuits richer. She baked them as Mrs. Bell had showed her.

NARRATOR 2: Clara smiled as she opened the lid of the Dutch oven to peek. Her biscuits were golden brown! It would be beans with hot biscuits for dinner tonight. The family gathered 'round.

SETH: I can't believe you made these biscuits!

READER 2 (as Ma): They look perfect!

READER 1 (as Edwin): What's he doing?

NARRATOR 3: Clara saw an Indian dressed in buckskin making his way from campfire to campfire. People at wagon after wagon turned him away. Then he walked toward Clara's wagon. He pointed to Clara's biscuits.

READER 3 (as the Indian): I am hungry.

NARRATOR 1: Clara was surprised he knew how to speak her language. She surely didn't know how to speak his. She handed him a hot biscuit on a plate.

NARRATOR 2: Clara set a can of molasses beside him. The Indian squatted on the ground. He poured molasses on the biscuit. Then he delicately pulled it apart with his fingers and ate it.

NARRATOR 3: The Indian pointed at the pan. Clara looked at Pa. He nodded. She gave the Indian the rest of the biscuits.

Next Page — **NARRATOR 1**

NARRATOR 1: He ate all but three. He tucked them into his buckskin shirt.

READER 3 (as the Indian): For hungry papooses.

NARRATOR 2: He stood up and looked at Pa.

READER 3 (as the Indian): Your family?

READER 1 (as Pa): Yes.

NARRATOR 3: The Indian shook hands with everyone, even Daniel. Then he looked sharply at Clara's family, as if to remember them.

READER 3 (as the Indian): Thank you.

NARRATOR 1: He mounted his pony and rode away. Iris held up the empty pan. She brushed an imaginary tear from her eye. They all laughed. A meal of beans and bacon with hard crackers would have to do.

NARRATOR 2: The next morning, the Morgan wagon led the wagon train. Each family took turns. It was less dusty at the front than farther back. Clara walked beside Pa and the oxen.

NARRATOR 3: Soon a long line of Indians appeared on the distant horizon. Their faces were painted. They yelled and shook their tomahawks as they rode closer.

NARRATOR 1: The wagon train halted. Men grabbed their rifles, ready to fight. A lone Indian suddenly appeared.

SOUND: [galloping pony]

Next Page — **NARRATOR 2**

NARRATOR 2: The Indian galloped his pony in front of the warriors with his hand raised. He must have been their leader, because the other Indians stopped. They turned and rode away.

READER I (as Pa): I don't know why, but I think just now we were powerful lucky.

CLARA: When will we reach Fort Laramie?

READER I (as Pa): In about three days. We'll stay a spell to do repairs and buy supplies. There's a doctor at the fort that your ma can see.

NARRATOR 3: Clara was glad that the Indians didn't show up again before they reached the fort.

NARRATOR I: Fort Laramie bustled with crowds of travelers, soldiers, and Indians. The family camped outside the fort. During supper, Clara saw an Indian coming toward them.

NARRATOR 2: The man wore beautifully beaded, creamy white buckskin. His feather headdress reached to his heels. A group of Indians followed him.

SETH: Don't you recognize him?

CLARA: The man who ate all our biscuits!

READER 3 (as the Indian): Friends.

NARRATOR 3: The Indian smiled. He shook hands solemnly with everyone again. Then he told Pa about a good place close by to hunt for elk.

Next Page — **NARRATOR I**

NARRATOR 1: After a few minutes, he raised his hand in a farewell gesture. He left, followed by the other Indians. A soldier standing nearby smiled.

READER 3 (as the soldier): Entertaining royalty, are you?

READER 1 (AS PA): What do you mean?

READER 3 (as the soldier): That man you were just talking to is a powerful Indian in these parts. He's one of the most respected leaders in the Sioux Nation. You could have a worse man for a friend.

NARRATOR 2: Pa and Clara looked at each other. Could that be the reason they hadn't been attacked a few days ago?

SETH: He's our friend because of Clara's biscuits!

NARRATOR 3: The soldier looked confused. Pa laughed.

READER 1 (as Pa): It's a long story.

NARRATOR 1: Two days later, while they were still at Fort Laramie, Clara's new baby sister arrived. Ma and Pa named her Evalina.

NARRATOR 2: On their last night at Fort Laramie, Clara pulled another pan of perfect biscuits off the fire. Ma was feeling better every day.

NARRATOR 3: Soon Ma would start cooking again. But Clara knew one thing for certain. No matter what, she would keep baking her lucky biscuits all the way to Oregon!

ALL: The End

Pronunciation Guide

Laramie: LAIR-uh-mee
papoose: pah-POOS
Platte: PLAT
Sioux: SOO

Glossary

beef jerky: strips of dried beef

buckskin: clothing made from the skin of a male deer

Dutch oven: a heavy iron cooking pot with a lid

elk: a large northern deer

Fort Laramie: a military post in eastern Wyoming that was a stop on the Oregon Trail

Great Plains: an area of flat, rolling grassland that covers much of central United States

hide: an animal's skin used to make leather

Indian Territory: land set aside within the United States for the use of American Indians

molasses: thick brown syrup made from sugarcane

papoose: an American Indian baby or young child

Platte River: a river in the Great Plains that the Oregon Trail followed for 450 miles

sacred: holy or deserving great respect

sagebrush: a silver-gray shrub that was sometimes used for fuel along the Oregon Trail

Sioux: the term white travelers used for the Lakota, a large group of American Indians who lived in the Great Plains

tomahawk: a small ax used as a weapon

wagon train: a group of covered wagons traveling together

Selected Bibliography

Clinkinbeard, Philura Vanderburgh, and Anna Dell Clinkinbeard. *Across the Plains in '64 by Prairie Schooner to Oregon.* New York: Exposition Books, 1953.

Mattes, Merrill J. *The Great Platte River Road: The Covered Wagon Mainline via Fort Kearney to Fort Laramie.* Lincoln: University of Nebraska Press, 1988.

Unruh, John D., Jr. *The Plains Across.* Urbana, IL: University of Chicago Press, 1979.

Wadsworth, Ginger. *Words West.* New York: Clarion Books, 2003.

Werner, Emmy E. *Pioneer Children on the Journey West.* Boulder, CO: Westview Press, 1995.

Williams, Jacqueline. *Wagon Wheel Kitchens.* Lawrence: University Press of Kansas, 1993.

Further Reading and Websites

BOOKS

Ichord, Loretta Frances. *Skillet Bread, Sourdough, and Vinegar Pie.* Minneapolis: Millbrook Press, 2003.
Learn more about cooking on the Oregon Trail. Tasty recipes are included.

Levine, Ellen. *. . . If You Traveled West in a Covered Wagon.* New York: Scholastic, 1986.
This book answers lots of questions about traveling in a covered wagon.

Levine, Michelle. *The Sioux.* Minneapolis: Lerner Publications Company, 2007.
Learn more about the history and culture of the American Indians who Clara's family met on their journey.

Moss, Marissa. *Rachel's Journal.* San Diego: Silver Whistle, 1998. Written in diary style, this book takes you along with an imaginary girl named Rachel on her travels on the Oregon Trail.

Van Leeuwen, Jean. *A Fourth of July on the Plains.* New York: Dial Books for Young Readers, 1997.
This story tells about a boy's idea for how the Fourth of July should be celebrated on the Oregon Trail.

WEBSITES

American Indian FAQ for Kids
http://www.native-languages.org/kidfaq.htm#1
This is a great site to find out facts about the different American Indian tribes and nations, and their cultures and traditions.

The Oregon Trail
http://americanhistory.pppst.com/oregontrail.html
This site has great PowerPoint presentations with pictures of many of the landmarks on the Oregon Trail.

The Oregon Trail
http://www.isu.edu/%7Etrinmich/Oregontrail.html
This is an informative site with many features, including facts about the Oregon Trail and archives of trail diaries and books.

Dear Teachers and Librarians,

Congratulations on bringing Reader's Theater to your students! Reader's Theater is an excellent way for your students to develop their reading fluency. Phrasing and inflection, two important reading skills, are at the heart of Reader's Theater. Students also develop public speaking skills such as volume, pacing, and facial expression.

The traditional format of Reader's Theater is very simple. There really is no right or wrong way to do it. By following these few tips, you and your students will be ready to explore the world of Reader's Theater.

EQUIPMENT

Location: A theater or gymnasium is a fine place for a Reader's Theater performance, but staging the performance in the classroom works well too.

Scripts: Each reader will need a copy of the script. Scripts that are individually printed should be bound into binders that allow the readers to turn the pages easily. Printable scripts for all the books in this series are available at www.lerneresource.com.

Music Stands: Music stands are very helpful for the readers to set their scripts on.

Costumes: Traditional Reader's Theater does not use costumes. Dressing uniformly, such as all wearing the same color shirt, will give a group a polished look. Specific costume pieces can be used when a reader is performing multiple roles. They help the audience follow the story.

Props: Props are optional. If necessary, readers may mime or gesture to convey objects that are important to the story. Props can be used much like a costume piece to identify different characters performed by one reader. Prop suggestions for each story are available at www.lerneresource.com.

Background and Sound Effects: These aren't essential, but they can add to the fun of Reader's Theater. Customized backgrounds for each story in this series and sound effects corresponding to the scripts are available at www.lerneresource.com. You will need a screen or electronic whiteboard for the background. You will need a computer with speakers to play the sound effects.

PERFORMANCE

Staging: Readers usually face the audience in a straight line or a semicircle. If the readers are using music stands, the stands should be raised chest high. A stand should not block a reader's mouth or face, but it should allow for the reader to read without looking down too much. The main character is usually placed in the center. The narrator is on the end. In the case of multiple narrators, place one narrator on each end.

Reading: Reader's Theater scripts do not need to be memorized. However, the readers should be familiar enough with the script to maintain a fair amount of eye contact with the audience. Encourage readers to act with their voices by reading with inflection and emotion.

Blocking (stage movement): For traditional Reader's Theater, there are no blocking cues to follow. You may want to have the students turn the pages simultaneously. Some groups prefer that readers sit or turn their backs to the audience when their characters are "offstage" or have left a scene. Some groups will have their readers move about the stage, script in hand, to interact with the other readers. The choice is up to you.

Overture and Curtain Call: Before the performance, a member of the group should announce the title and the author of the piece. At the end of the performance, all readers step in front of their music stands, stand in a line, grasp hands, and bow in unison.

Please visit www.lerneresource.com for printable scripts, prop suggestions, sound effects, a background image that can be projected on a screen or electronic whiteboard, a Reader's Theater teacher's guide, and reading-level information for all roles.